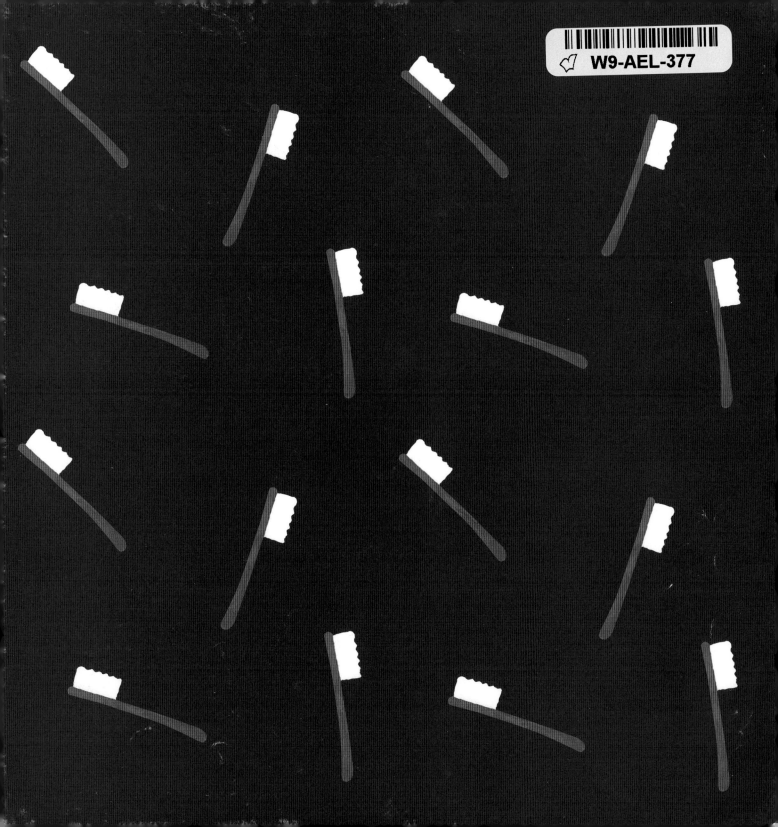

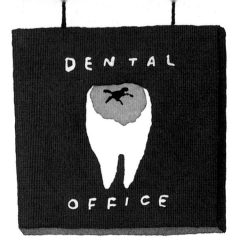

First Chronicle Books LLC edition published in the United States of America in 2018.
Originally published in Japan in 1984 by KAISEI-SHA Publishing Co., Ltd. under the title *Wanisan Doki' Haishasan Doki.'*

Copyright © 1984 by Taro Gomi.
English translation copyright © 2018 by Chronicle Books LLC.
English translation rights arranged with KAISEI-SHA Publishing Co., Ltd. through Japan Foreign-Rights Centre.

Library of Congress Cataloging-in-Publication Data available.

ISBN 978-1-4521-7028-2

Manufactured in China.

Typeset in Steagal Rough.

10 9 8 7 6 5 4 3 2 1

Chronicle Books LLC
680 Second Street
San Francisco, California 94107

Chronicle Books—we see things differently.
Become part of our community at www.chroniclekids.com.

The **Crocodile** and the **Dentist**

Taro Gomi

chronicle books·san francisco

I really don't want to . . .

. . . but I have to.

I really don't want to,
but I have to.

Must I?

Must I?

I'm scared . . .

But I should be brave.

But I should be brave.

I'm ready for the worst!

I'm ready for the worst!

What an **awful** thing to do!

What an **awful** thing to do!

There's no use
getting angry.

There's no use getting angry.

Just a little longer . . .

Just a little longer . . .

Whew...

Whew...

Thank you so much.
See you again next year!

Thank you so much.
See you again next year!

I don't want to see him again!

So I must remember
to brush my teeth!

G. TARO.

So you must remember
to brush your teeth!